To my grandparents,
and to everyone who is missing someone.

Library of Congress Cataloging-in-Publication Data Available
ISBN 978-1-338-68069-0 · 10 9 8 7 6 5 4 3 2 1   21 22 23 24 25
Printed in China 38 · First edition, October 2021
Jocelyn Li Langrand's artwork was created digitally. · The text type was set in KG Primary Penmanship and the display type was hand lettered by Jocelyn Li Langrand.
The book was printed on 140gsm Golden Sun woodfree paper and bound at RR Donnelley Asia.
Production was overseen by Catherine Weening.
Manufacturing was supervised by Shannon Rice.
The book was art directed and designed by Doan Buu and edited by Jess Harold.

if
YOU
MiSS
me

by

JOCELYN LI LANGRAND

Orchard Books
An Imprint of Scholastic Inc.
New York

Charlie loved to dance,
and her grandma loved to watch her.

She watched her in class,
on the playground,

and all through town.

At night, Charlie and Grandma danced
under the moonlight,

or, if they were tired,
made wishes to the moon about their hearts' desire.

When fall came, Charlie moved
to the city with her parents.
Grandma said, "If you miss me,
look at the moon. I will do the same."

Sometimes, Grandma came to the city.

There, she watched Charlie dance with her friends.

Charlie's heart always
leaped when she saw
Grandma in the crowd.

Each time Grandma left, she said, "If you miss me, look at the moon. I will do the same."

Sometimes, they
talked on the phone.
Charlie loved to share every
detail of her dances with
Grandma, and Grandma wanted to
hear them all.

"I have a dance recital this
summer," said Charlie.
"Will you come?"

"I will be there,"
Grandma promised.

But when winter came,
Grandma visited Charlie less and less.
It was Charlie's turn to visit during break.

"I miss you, Grandma, when will you come to
see me dance again?" Charlie asked.
"Don't worry," Grandma said. "If you miss me,
look at the moon..."
Charlie finished her sentence, "I will do the same."
Then she asked, "Why the moon?"

"Because even if we're apart," Grandma said,
"the same moon shines for both of us.
So when I see the moon, I see you."

Not long after that, Grandma passed away.

It was the coldest winter Charlie ever remembered.

It was the hardest one, too.
Charlie kept making mistakes during practice.

Dancing was not the same
without Grandma.

In truth, nothing was the same without Grandma.

But at night, the moon whispered to Charlie.
It sounded like, "I miss you, too."

For the next few weeks, Charlie danced every day after school, preparing with her dance studio for the summer recital.

It was the biggest show of the year,

and Charlie wished to dance her best.

Dancing
Moon

Dancing
Moon

THEATER

SUMMER SHOW
DANCING ON THE MOON
START AT 7:00 PM

Soon, it was time.
Everyone arrived
excited for the
big night.

TICKETS

Everyone except for Charlie, who felt
nervous and alone like never before.

She didn't search the crowd for familiar
faces this time. Instead, she looked up.

Charlie's heart leaped!

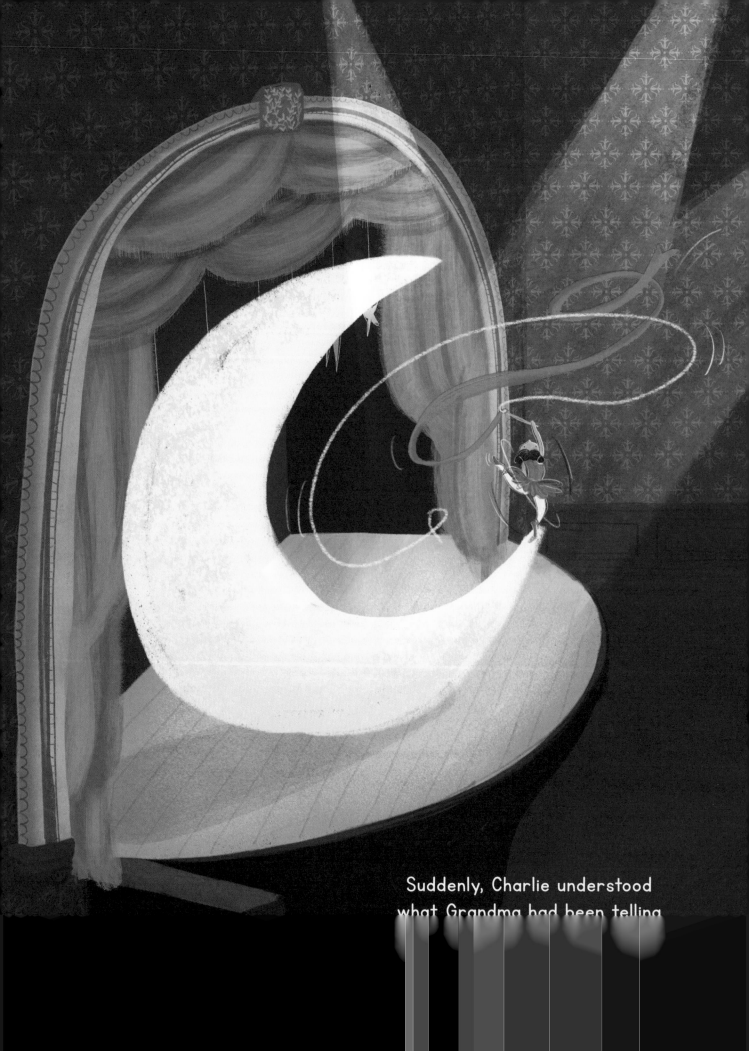

Suddenly, Charlie understood
what Grandma had been telling

Even if she and Grandma were apart, the same moon shined for both of them.

So when Charlie saw the moon,

she saw Grandma, too.